"If I were a killer, would it matter?" His mouth was closer than I expected as he dipped his head. I gasped, and he ran his nose against mine.

"No, it wouldn't," I breathed like a twisted confession.

USA TODAY BESTSELLING AUTHOR

Lynessa Layne

Cover by Lynessa Layne

Images courtesy of Shutterstock

Story originally featured in the Flirty in Kansas City Anthology

Also by Lynessa Layne

The Don't Close Your Eyes Series

Killer Kiss – a novelette

Don't Close Your Eyes

Complicated Moonlight

Mad Love

Dangerous Games

Hostile Takeover

Target Acquired

Point Blank

Short Stories

The Getaway

Winter in Roatan

Whispers Through the Trees

The Crow's Nest

Magazine Articles

The Villains of Romantic Suspense

Character Point of View

♂ = Klive King

♀ = Kinsley Hayes

A DON'T CLOSE YOUR EYES NOVELETTE

KILLER KISS

USA TODAY BESTSELLING AUTHOR

Lynessa Layne

Part One

"**ATTENTION ALL PASSENGERS** OF flight 1324 to Tampa, please make your way to gate C54. Boarding will begin shortly."

"Hallelujah. About time." I unplugged my phone from the community charging station, capped my water bottle and shuffled my boarding pass under my arm as my screen lit with a call.

"Hello?" I answered, then pinched the device between my chin and shoulder.

"Well, Kinsley," Julie said. "It's been an hour. Did you think about it?"

"The only thing I can think about is getting on this plane," I muttered.

"I'm serious," she said. "You asked for an hour to think it over, I gave you an hour."

I glanced at the wall clock. "On the dot, not a second to spare, eh?"

"I don't have any spare seconds. Please."

I rubbed my lips together and shoved my water bottle into a side pocket on my backpack. "I dunno, Jules ...."

"Come on! *Please* come! Eliza has strep throat; she can't attend. She can barely speak." Julie pleaded her case while I half-listened to updates about flight delays and arrivals and watched my plane creep toward the gate.

"I hate hearing she's sick." I adjusted the backpack on my shoulder and phone into my palm, stepping closer to the window.

"Is that a yes?" Julie asked. "You're the perfect substitute for her role. Do I really need to beg a bestie?"

"Nice. Julie, am I the killer?"

A small child gasped. I grinned as I turned my back on the boy and side-stepped a man playing on his phone.

"I can't tell you that." Julie popped her gum. "Even the killer doesn't know they're the killer. That's the whole concept of a murder mystery dinner."

"You've lost your mind. You seriously want me to drag in straight off my flight and play Eliza's role when I haven't even seen a script? A) I'm not a performing arts major or even *minor*. B) Didn't she say her character makes-out in a coat closet with a total stranger? A stranger who, by the way, might be the killer if I'm not?"

"It's for a good cause!" she spoke over my reasoning. "Kinsley, I've spent the whole semester putting this together! This is important for the drama department! I even snagged a socialite who donated like ten grand!"

"What's in it for the socialite?"

"You ask too many questions."

"You don't answer enough," I quipped, but grinned to myself with her unamused expression in my mind.

She cleared her throat. "Eliza thinks he's paying to make-out with some hot college chick. Since you're a notorious bitch on campus you might need someone who's paying. A favor for a favor."

"Ha!" I cackled too loud by mistake. "You need to hush! Have you seen this socialite?"

"No."

"Has Eliza? Is that why she's suddenly sick?"

She popped a bubble. "You'll have to ask her when you call to check on her health and thank her for this unexpected opportunity. The donor preferred confidentiality. He will be sporting a red handkerchief, or whatever those breast pocket decorations are."

"You mean a pocket square?" I asked, unable to fight a wry grin.

"Sure," she said, popped another bubble.

"What if he's gross?" I asked. "What do I get for taking one for the team?"

She scoffed. "What if he's hot and you meet *the one* because of me? You'll end up married to a socialite and you can forever tell your snobby friends that I introduced you."

I mistakenly laughed too loud again and apologized to those around me. "What if I just pretend I made-out with this guy? Aren't we all masked up anyway? How will anyone know if we've been kissing without us telling them?"

"Kinsley, you know the mask policy isn't in effect here. The venue is in a hotel next to the airport. Shuttle and everything. You can change when you arrive."

"Change into what?" I snapped my fingers. "I left my flapper dress in my great grandmother's trunk. Wished you said something sooner."

"Smart-ass. I'm not asking you to be a flapper."

"Nah, just to flap gums with a stranger during a pandemic. No biggie."

She sighed. "Please. I know it's a huge ask."

I dropped all sarcasm. "Julie, I was supposed to arrive in Tampa this morning. My flight was bumped, and my father rescheduled his whole day to pick me up when I arrive. If I call him for yet *another* change in plans, he'll get pissy, especially if I divulge the role you're begging me to play. Don't actors typically have understudies for situations like this?"

The doors to the gate flooded with exhausted passengers departing the plane. I couldn't wait to board! Everyone always looked so grumpy, but I loved flying. Well, except for now.

"Ugh. Fine." Julie sighed. "You leave me no choice but to confess. There is no understudy, because I called your parents and invited them to donate. They were thrilled to join and volunteered you. Your dad wanted it to be a surprise. Your mother's bringing you a dress she says is perfect."

"Wow." I paused to absorb this insanity. "My dad knows about the kissing?"

"Meh ... not exactly ... he knows you've kissed a guy before, right? Like, he won't make a thing of it?"

I practically saw her cringe in my mind while I mirrored the image. "Define *thing*," I joked. Now I worried if I couldn't make this flight, my parents would miss out on the surprise family date they'd planned. I told Julie as much.

"Like you always say, let the chips fall where they may?" she asked, a little uncertain. "When are you landing?"

"In about an hour," I grumbled, suddenly as crabby as those jostling my backpack on their way to baggage claim. Performing with jet lag should be interesting.

"Attention all passengers of flight 1324 to Tampa, we apologize for earlier weather delays. We will now begin boarding. First class passengers, please promptly line up at gate C54 with your boarding passes ready, business class ...." The attendants crammed hasty instructions through a loudspeaker muffled by their masks.

"Gotta go, Jules." More than first class rushed to board. "They're rushing coach aboard on the heels of business class to make up for earlier delays. I'll be there with lipstick on."

She squealed with delight and laid out the details faster than I followed.

"Jules. Text me the info. My section's being called." I disconnected and scurried into the line. The man playing on his phone dashed in line behind me while I handed my boarding pass to the attendant.

"Good evening, Kinsley." She smiled after reading my pass and identification. "Will you pull your face covering down for a second?" I followed her instructions. She played match game with my features, nodded, then scanned my pass. A red light flashed instead of green.

"No, no, no," I whined. "Please, I've already been bumped once, and I have plans."

"Replace your mask over your mouth and nose, please, Miss. I apologize. Seems your stand-by ticket was bumped for a family traveling together. We have three business class tickets available if you'd like to upgrade, otherwise you will need to wait for the next available flight."

I shook my head, replaced my face covering and took my ticket from her. She extended another hollow apology after I asked why they didn't feel the need to page me ahead of time so I could adjust my plans.

"It's fine." Not *fine*. I headed for the concierge to resolve the problem. Eight hours in Atlanta Hartsfield-Jackson International Airport now frayed my nerves. If I'd rented a car when I'd landed here earlier, I'd already be in Tampa.

I slapped the ticket on the counter. Julie's phone went straight to voicemail when I called. Not good. "Jules, you're gonna have to call someone else to be the murdering make-out queen for your dinner. ATL bumped me *again.* I'm never flying stand—"

"Two business class tickets immediately, please?" A man's stern voice made me jump aside. The one who'd played with his phone earlier.

"I'm so sorry," I told him and grabbed my ID off the counter. He didn't look the type to entertain fools or delays to his schedule. All business. I mumbled to Julie's voicemail as he spoke to the booking agent.

"Hang up," he told me. I did what he said out of impulsive respect. Instead of an explanation for why he'd cut in line, he handed me a ticket and ordered me to hurry. "Come now, we haven't much time." He gestured around our empty gate. Rather than argue, I shoved the boarding pass at the attendant. She greeted me again, asked me to show my face for another identification check, told me to promptly replace the covering and wished me a wonderful flight as if she'd not kicked me to the curb minutes ago. The man's hand went to the small of my back to rush me through the deserted jet way since I was still confused.

"Hi, Kinsley. Don't panic. I got your name from the pass and identification you had on the counter. Also, it sounded as though you needed an alibi for this evening." His eyes smiled down at me. *Jeez, that's what I get for airing my business in public.*

"I can't pay for this ticket," I stammered.

"I don't want you to, nor am I asking you to. Ever hear of a good deed?" he asked.

"Oh, gosh, that's quite the good deed. Thank you so much!"

"You're welcome. The next flight to Tampa is on the opposite side of the airport in thirty minutes. Atlanta is a nightmare to cross without more than an hour. Is that what happened to your original flight today?"

"I was visiting family in Tennessee, and they'd bought my tickets. I didn't realize my returning flight was a stand-by rate until it was too late."

"You from Tennessee? I don't hear that particular twang in your voice."

"No. I live in Tampa. You?" I asked but got cut off when the flight attendants greeted us like we were a couple. My instinct was to beeline for the last rows on the airplane. My new friend tugged my backpack to stop me just two rows after first class. The people behind our curtain lounged in luxury leather, two to a row instead of three miniature seats cramped together.

"Would you like the window?" the man asked. "May I stow your knapsack?"

"S-sure, thank you." I double-checked my pass while shrugging out of the straps. "This is my seat?" I pointed and looked over my shoulder as the tall man closed the overhead compartment with our things inside. *Short person bonus!*

A balding blimp of a man in the seat next to mine huffed behind his mask and fogged his face shield.

"I'm sorry," I told him.

The man who'd paid for my ride cleared his throat. "Forgive the inconvenience, sir. Would there be any reason we couldn't swap seats so I may sit with my wife?"

My cheeks filled with blood at the intimacy of the title when I was only twenty-three-years-old. The hefty man glared at me. I bit my lip and stared at the floor while he shoved out of his seat, annoyance on full display.

"I assure you this is more for your comfort than my own pleasure," my companion explained. "She gets plane-sick sometimes. Miss!" He flagged the attendant. "Would you be so kind as to bring extra barf bags in case of emergency?"

My eyes bugged. At this time in history, wasn't that akin to saying *bomb* in an airplane? The attendant nodded in gross alarm and turned on her heel.

The heavy man ripped his arms back like I'd already vomited and had some on my shirt, then sank gratefully down into the opposite aisle seat.

"You trying to get me booted from another flight?" I hissed under my breath. The handsome man chuckled to himself as I took my spot. He elegantly smoothed his blazer and took the seat beside me.

"Your bickering and glare make our relationship more believable; don't you think?" he said near my ear. Flutters filled my belly for the briefest moment.

I smiled under my mask. "The way your mask fogs your glasses really hits that married man look home."

He nodded and chuckled. "I hate these masks." He pulled his glasses to clean the steam with his tie.

"Why not wear contacts?" I asked. When I looked into his green eyes, I could've sworn I saw the almost invisible rim of contact lenses. Weird!

The flight attendant returned with the barf bags and a ginger ale for added measure. Unable to resist a return dig, I looked at my pretend husband and said, "Honey, I know you hate the masks, but you can't see a thing without your glasses. Please, put them back on. I don't want you to accidentally spill my soda."

He flared his eyes— yep, contact lens rims around his irises— and returned the black rims to his face, then reached across me. "Here, darling. Keep the shade open. You know that always helps."

"Aw, you're so thoughtful," I said, "and that's what I love about you." I fought a smile at the way his eyes lit and how the flight attendant warmed toward us. When she left, my awe rushed out on a pleased sigh as I placed my drink into a cup-holder, buckled-up and took in the private screen with complimentary earbuds.

A dinner menu tucked into the seat back along with a schedule of available movies. An attendant pulled the cabin door closed and sealed us inside. The screens before us flashed. A video of the procedures and exit strategies played. I stretched my petite frame to relish the legit foot space and the ability to recline. I wished this flight were longer to indulge in this luxury. I marveled at the level of service our tiny section already received.

"Your reverie is showing." The man's full attention landed on my face. "Would I travel this way without my wife being accustomed to such accommodation?"

My eyebrow arched. "Would you really marry someone so ungrateful?"

He hummed and looked at his royal dinner menu. I noticed a platinum band on his left ring finger, tiny onyx stone beside an amethyst.

"Touché," he said. "Perhaps this is why we eloped during a drunken fling. You weren't my type, but you made me realize my type wasn't right."

I rolled my eyes and pulled my own menu. "Is that how you met your real wife? I doubt she'd be pleased with your flirting with me."

"I'm not married," he said quietly with a look around us, so he didn't ruin our act.

"What's with the ring?" I pointed.

"Would you believe me if I said I was committed to someone I'm not yet with? This is my deterrent to anyone who shows an interest."

My mouth dropped, though he couldn't see. "No way. I don't believe you."

"I swear it." His eyes remained fixed.

"Like a promise ring situation?"

"Of sorts, yes, though less for religious conviction and more for personal discipline. When I make up my mind, it's set, and I'm set on one woman."

This time I didn't feign my awe. "That is the sweetest thing. Are you dating her?"

"I'd love to, but life as it is does not permit such luxury. I hope to do so in the future. I'm working toward that goal."

"Hold on." I leaned against the window to see him better. The plane bucked as the tug pushed us in reverse. "You're not dating her, but you're committed to her? Is she committed to you, too?"

"Shh." He looked around again and lowered his hand, so I'd lower my voice. "You'll give us away. Ever hear of unrequited love?"

I almost choked on my own laugh. "*You* unrequited?" I pulled my mask down to give him a peek at my shock. "Now I know you're pulling my leg."

"I'm telling the truth. Honest."

"Say I believe you. How could she not return your love when, *if* you're telling the truth, she'd be the luckiest girl?"

"Oh, you think she's lucky, do you? I'm flattered." His smile was shy. Mine was adoring. If he wore his Clark Kent glasses for appearances, I saw why. They added a softness to his firm demeanor. "The two of us have spent a little over five minutes together tonight, which is about fifteen minutes less than I spent with her when I fell ass over tit."

Laughter burst through my mask at his idiom. I'd never heard an American say that before. I said so. He looked at his tray table.

"I'm a fan of British television. Sometimes their vernacular bleeds into my speech," he said. He did have a particular propriety in his elocution. Made sense. His fingers flicked beside his temple. "Fun fact, I even think with a British accent," he said with a British accent.

"Impressive impression," I said with a British accent of my own.

"As is yours!"

"So." I cleared the play accent. "You spent twenty minutes with her before you fell ass over tit and then what happened? Too bad they don't have popcorn to go with this unfolding drama."

"For business class, they do. When we finish taxiing, I'll request some for you."

"Aw, you really are thoughtful!" I whined in animation like a silly girl. He was fun to make smile, even if all I could see was the crinkling of his eyes and little puffs of steam at the bottoms of his fake glasses.

"I asked her out and she said no."

Again, my jaw dropped behind my mask. "What is the matter with her? Why waste your time wearing that ring for someone who rejected you?"

He shrugged. "The timing was off. We didn't meet under the most natural of circumstances. I was really clumsy with my words."

My hands cupped at my chest. "But you're like a hot dork. Hot dorks are supposed to be clumsy with their words. It's part of your charm."

His head tilted while his Adam's apple bobbed through a bashful laugh. "Ah, thank you, I guess? Nice to know you think I'm hot and dorky. I'll take it." He pulled his glasses and wiped the steam with his tie again. "I've seen her a few times since our initial meeting. Once, I even bought her coffee, but she didn't seem to recall me. That, and I didn't own up to being the buyer. I haven't spoken to her in a little over a year."

"You just silently watch the world go by with her in it?" I couldn't help slapping his arm. "Women aren't mind readers! You're saving yourself for someone who doesn't even know you love her? Ugh! You're killing me, Smalls! Why don't you try again?"

"You think I should? I'd probably fail miserably again. I haven't improved in the grace department, especially where she's concerned. Every time I see her, I have a hard time breathing. For now, I blame the masks, but what happens when they come off and I'm left wide open with the truth on display?"

"Were you wearing a mask when you met her?"

"Kind of."

"Take it off."

"And get us booted from this flight? We'd have to get a hotel overnight."

I tsked at his play. "I'm serious."

"In all sincerity," he said, "as I told you, life doesn't permit me to unmask myself or have a relationship right now."

"Then you need a life change, bud. Let me guess, lawyer? Too dedicated to your career?"

The pilot came over the intercom with an apology for the crowded runway and their effort to communicate with air traffic control for an estimate on departure.

"Not a lawyer," my new friend said, "but I know enough law to keep myself out of trouble."

"Enough that we can get an annulment after we land?" I teased. "I can't be with a man who's in love with another woman."

"I'd offer you your freedom, darling, but law states you are ineligible for an annulment if you've consummated the relationship."

I laughed too loud at that one. "Nice. How quickly your commitment wanes. I'm not part of the Mile High club, sir. You should quit your job if it's taking you away from her."

"I've thought of opening dialog to assess her feelings while I still have my job, but my work is complicated. It's not the sort of job you have as a married man."

"Ooh lala ...." I rubbed my palms together. "Like a spy?" *May explain the fake glasses and contacts ... was his hair truly the color of wet sand? His eyebrows were almost black ....*

He laughed full and hearty and took my hand like a husband would. The hot dork held my fingers in his upon his open tray table as the flight attendant delivered glasses of champagne. He politely accepted but asked if he could have a Captain and Coke as well. My heart fluttered to my throat.

"I'm sorry, sir. We don't have Captain Morgan, but we do have Bacardi. Will that be acceptable?"

I chewed my lip beneath my mask. Captain Morgan painted memories of the sexy pirate I'd met after the Gasparilla festival last year. I should cut this hot dork some slack because I knew too well what wanting someone you'd met once was like.

Where this guy was shy and cute, that one had been domineering and British with stormy gray eyes and a grip that could make you go limp, so he'd have to hold you like a Harlequin cover. I nearly shuddered in my seat recalling the sensations he'd infused just touching my waist.

"Bacardi is fine," my friend said.

"And for your wife?" Her hand gestured toward me. I snapped out of my daydreams of another man like the cheating spouse I wasn't.

"This is excellent," I said. "Thank you."

"If it wouldn't be too much trouble, might we have a bag of popcorn at your earliest convenience?" he asked. When she left, I drew my mask down to thank him for the popcorn before I indulged in the delicious alcohol, all with one hand because he hadn't released my other yet. "I can't believe we get champagne. Mmm … this is pretty good!"

"I'm glad you like it. You may have mine when you've finished your own."

"Ha! Not if I want to walk straight when we land."

He leaned forward to see outside the window. We shared the view of nine other planes waiting to depart ahead of ours. The sky was dark, and all the runway lights glowed beneath the flashing lights on the planes' wings.

"Judging by that line, I'd say you have time for a whole bottle. Hope your plans won't be ruined."

"Same to you." I looked over my shoulder, about two inches from his face, and swallowed. "I think you should make a move while you still have your job. Be brave. Courage is hard to find in men these days. You'll stand out and she'll never forget you. Trust me."

"Oh?" he asked, his soft eyes studying what he could of my face under the covering and the lights that went dim in the cabin. The plane moved and we nearly bumped masks.

"Attention passengers," the pilot's crackly voice said. "We've just received permission to move to the front of the line and will take flight here in about four minutes. Please fasten your seatbelts. Flight attendants prepare for departure."

Part Two

KINSLEY AND I SAT **back in our seats** as the plane's gravitational force pressed us against the leather. She squeezed my hand holding hers. I relished every second of lightning striking twice for us. Just over a year ago, I'd crossed paths with a scorned ginger crying herself into a fit on the night of Gasparilla. Because of her, I was late to the festival and the hit I'd had to execute.

This evening, the private plane I chartered for dirty work had a mechanical issue, so I booked a last-minute flight on the first airline heading back to Tampa. Figures I'd be in disguise yet again, but what a wonderful opportunity to speak to the woman who, by her own definition, was lucky to have my love? Tonight, I was the lucky one and she never the wiser.

She was quiet as the plane climbed in altitude. I looked out the window with her at the cloud cover. Her hand squeezed harder when we hit turbulence. Her other held an empty champagne flute she'd pinned to her chest.

"It's normal when traveling through storm clouds," I said. "They're climbing high enough to fly over the danger rather than through it." The pilot echoed as much a second later while warning the cabin to keep our seatbelts fastened.

"I hate turbulence," she said. Her arms nearly flew around my neck when the plane dropped. The passengers cried out while I quietly held her through the next five minutes of bumper cars. "The wings are bouncing!" She gripped my tie, I think by mistake, unless she wanted to choke me this time around, although so far, I was doing a better job speaking to her than last time.

"That's normal. They're made to flex with the wind. It's all going to be okay." I patted her rigid back and ran my nails up and down her cotton tee-shirt. "Do you know what I think?"

"What?" she asked, her speech muffled against my chest. Kinsley's sloppy bun tickled my nose as her hair moved with our plane.

"I think I'm the luckiest man in that airport. Of the lottery of passengers to be seated with, I've won."

Her grip on my tie eased as her face crept from hiding to peer into my eyes. "You kind of cheated by buying me this seat, but I think that's the sweetest compliment. Thank you."

After minutes of smooth air, she braved a look out at what I loved: the stars above a carpet of clouds. Lightning flashed below us. Her fingers tightened on my forearm, but gradually she relaxed until finally sitting back in her seat.

The pilot came over the intercom. "Attention passengers, we've reached a cruising altitude of thirty-six-thousand feet. Looks like smooth skies for the remainder of our trip to Tampa. For those not familiar with the destination, you may find some R&R on the white sand of Clearwater Beach ....." The pilot droned on about Tampa's various tourist destinations that made blending in so easy. Our flight attendant returned with a bag of freshly popped popcorn.

Kinsley's eyes crinkled and met mine. *Anything you want, love, especially if you look at me with those eyes.* Before I fell into an accidental staring contest, I opened the bag for her and said, "I've indulged you in my drama. Now that we have popcorn, indulge me in yours. What was this murder I overheard you talking about on the phone?"

"Oh, that?" She waved her hand and grabbed a piece of popcorn, slid the bite under her mask. "Ever heard of a murder mystery dinner? My friend, Julie, is a drama major. She put this event together to raise money for the department. I didn't plan to go, but basically guests dress up like whatever theme is chosen and we try solving a crime using clues and actors she's planted into the setting of a real dinner. She swears not even the killer knows they're the killer."

"Intriguing," I told her. "Sounds fun to me, then again I enjoy any opportunity to cosplay. You didn't seem too jazzed about going."

"Jazzed?" she asked. "Careful, your age is showing."

"Burn!"

"Your drink, sir. And a refill on champagne. I'm sorry about the delay and earlier turbulence." The attendant handed me the drink I'd ordered to jog Kinsley's memory. She looked beyond me to Kinsley, passed her the fresh flute. "I hope you're feeling okay."

I tugged my mask to my chin and tipped the liquor and cola to my lips to keep from laughing at Kinsley's confirmation of feeling fine now. We watched her leave.

Kinsley ripped her mask down like she could wait no longer. She drained half her glass before saying, "I have to kiss a stranger." Her face sobered. "My father is going. If I can even make myself kiss this guy, how will I sell it with him there? Julie wants passion to sell an intrinsic part of the plot. I'm horrible at faking. There's no way."

I worked my hand, swirling my drink.

"How scary," I said like a smart-ass. "Do you think daddy's going to beat him up because you kissed the man?"

Her hand slapped my arm while she laughed and said, "I'm not kidding. I care what he thinks of me."

"I'd be less concerned about your father and more concerned for yourself. You are an adult I hope, otherwise I'm going to have to trade seats with that guy again to keep myself from being arrested for marrying a minor and providing her alcohol."

She chortled and took a sip from her flute. "I thought you knew your law. Depending on where we got married, you'd become my guardian and I could legally drink with your consent but thank goodness I'm twenty-three and you're in the clear."

"Make it your business to know a lot about alcohol, do you?"

"I'm a bartender. If you'd have bothered getting to know me before marriage, you'd have known how low you were slumming."

This bloody woman. She was too easy to think of as my wife. "I'm a pathetic cliché."

"Are you wealthy? Because that would also make me a cliché for marrying a hot dork for his money."

I imagined taking her to the lavatory for a honeymoon when I nodded.

She nodded with me. "So is this hot-shot donor I'm supposed to make-out with. That's a lot of pressure." She filled me in on her friend claiming this bloke was paying to make-out with a hot college girl. "What if she's right?" Kinsley asked. "What if he's so gross he's willing to donate ten-thousand dollars to get someone to kiss him? I told her I could pretend. You know? Maybe smack my lips to look like they were kissed? Mess up his hair and mine?"

I'd love nothing more than to dig my hands into her hair and snap the elastic holding her bun in place.

"Pretending isn't a bad idea given your hesitance." I lifted her mask back over her lips like I'd done so for the flight attendant when really, I couldn't handle the pictures she painted. "Refills for both of us, please?" I asked the flight attendant, then turned back to her covered mouth. "If this man—assuming it's a man—is a wretched kisser you don't want to wound him with your disgust."

Her eyes bulged with such animation, I laughed.

"See there? That won't do. You'll have him storming out of the place in a tiff and there goes your friend's money."

"This is a bad idea. You're right. If I don't go through with this, she might lose her donation."

I raised my eyebrows. "That's a *lot* of money riding on your ability to kiss. Given your attachment to your daddy, I take it you've not kissed many men. This is a dangerous predicament you've gotten yourself into."

"Asshole," she whispered playfully. *There's my girl.* "I've kissed a handful of guys and none of them ever complained about anything other than not passing Go. I'll take that as a good sign that they liked the way I kissed, thank you."

"Or they wanted to bypass the bad part to get to the good part."

She slapped my arm and told me to behave. "What if he's got a long tongue, or too much spit? Rich guys don't do well with honesty. They're egocentric because no one tells them the truth."

"Is that so? We've establishing that I'm wealthy. Does that mean my peers lie while I gain fulfillment from their inflation?"

Her whole face fell. She cursed under her breath.

"Calm yourself, I'm only playing, darling. Your fears are legitimate. I'd dread being in your shoes, but what if this poor guy dreads the same about you? That's a pretty penny to pay for a make-out session with a girl who might not be hot at all or who can't kiss well. What if you don't even realize *your* tongue is too long, or your mouth produces too much saliva? These masks we're wearing breed bad breath and you've been marinating all day."

She slapped a hand over her mask and begged with her eyes to know if her breath was bad. I laughed for the umpteenth time in a row. By far, the most I'd laughed in a great while.

"I hadn't thought of that ...." she whispered, afraid.

The refills came. The attendant appeared alarmed by Kinsley's expression.

"She's fine," I assured her. Kinsley peered unseeingly at her drink, deflated. "Consider this,

Kinsley. If you pretend and refuse to kiss your partner, he could become one of two things: relieved he doesn't have to fake it with you, or disappointed because you turned out to be such a child about it, afraid of the big bad man. Tricky decision to make. Which is the worse of the evils?"

Amazing someone so pretty could be made to feel so inadequate. *Should I rescue her? Revive her fire?*

"You know, if you needed a non-biased third party to give an honest critique, we haven't landed for our annulment yet. I'm still married to you for thirty more minutes."

"Ha!" Her eyes lit and crinkled. "Nice try. There is a chance my partner could become so infatuated with kissing me that his hands roam where they shouldn't and no longer for the sake of the role, but because he's an awful pervert. That leads to stalkers, then Dad's pulling the shotgun. It could become a bloodbath. Probably best to avoid the entire situation." She turned and snapped up the package of earbuds after a self-satisfied sip of her drink.

Now, *that*'s the girl who'd stolen my sanity without any idea. As she found the movie she wanted on the touch screen, I tamed my mile-high desires and sipped my fresh Bacardi and Coke.

When we disembarked, Kinsley added polite space between us without appearing like we hadn't been together. We walked in companionable silence until she tossed a small wave, a shy, "thanks again," then slinked between a group of women into the lavatory. My pace didn't falter.

The heavyset man who'd traded seats with me hitched a ride on a cart. As he passed by, he grunted his confirmed suspicion. I smiled to myself. If he knew the real relationship I had with Kinsley Hayes, he'd have ordered his own popcorn and leaned forward in his chair to hear more.

Once in baggage claim, I parked myself before the carousel praying my bag made the trip with me. Though I couldn't wait to change out of this disguise, I'd just paid thirteen-hundred dollars in upgraded tickets to have a single hour with her all to myself; a few more hours in the name of borrowed time with the girl I loved wouldn't hurt.

Kinsley came off the escalator removing her mask just as I spotted my bag. I removed my mask, too, and hoisted the heavy suitcase from the others. When I pulled the handle to wheel the luggage, I caught her eyes on me.

She looked down too late and blushed. When she braved another look at me, I dug into my pocket and wiggled a little something before tossing the breath spray her way. She lunged to catch my offering and frowned when she read the label.

I blew a kiss, smiled, and mouthed, *good luck*, before walking out of the airport with plans to press my tux and buy a ticket to her friend's mystery dinner as the only true killer in attendance.

Part Three

CHAMPAGNE FIZZLED IN MY flute as I speculated who in this ballroom committed murder. If anyone suspected *me*, I'd yet to notice, though my effort to remember the few lines Julie had given me when I was dressing likely made me appear nervous. I mingled, eavesdropping on others' conversations. My foot fanned the trail of my dress back where the purple satin belonged.

Stupid gown.

Yards away, my mother lifted her chin, so I'd lift mine, then discreetly motioned I keep the slit in my dress from showing too much thigh. I shook my head, tempted to allow the eye-full for her audacity in bringing such attire and forcing me to walk on pins and needles with stilettos so thin!

She cheated in her high heels by holding my father's arm in his tux and basked in beauty queen bliss as she floated about the room like thanking judges for crowning her. While everyone dressed in formal elegance, Mom toyed with a cockiness far beyond her normal demeanor. *Hmm ... character trait for Julie or was she the murderer?*

I sipped from my flute, feeling a little more mature about kissing even a gross guy if I'd had enough to drink. My free fingers sorted numerous photos of the victim and the crime scene scattered across a central table. Other attendees carried notepads with pens, questioning witnesses and writing every detail. After taking orders at the bar for years, I'd long since dumped the pad and memorized verbal and social cues; probably didn't help my case. Didn't make my mother look innocent either.

Rather than take notes or ask questions, she worked the room as if my father and I cooped her up in our home rather than exhausted ourselves with her social events. *Hold on ... had Mom played a role in the actual event-planning?*

If so, my make-out partner better be hot!

"Evening, darling."

I ripped around just as something velvet soft dragged across my bare shoulders. Champagne burned my nostrils as I snorted by mistake. "Holy shit." I choked and beat my chest to clear my clogged airway.

The hot dork from my flight looked me straight in the eyes without a polite look away, watching and waiting for me to finish, a different air about him here when we weren't sitting. At last, I cleared my throat. My cheeks felt as red as the little rose boutonniere he handed me. Hot dork looked more like Clark Kent meets James Bond. Maybe he *was* a spy because he carried no notes, either, but snagged a champagne flute from a nearby tray and seamlessly stole my glass from my fingers, replacing the empty with his new offering.

He leaned in and kissed my cheek while his fingertips whispered against my waist. My heart snared in my ears, and I inhaled his spicy fragrance like seasoning for the yummy meal he was sure to be were I the type to snack on whatever I wanted whenever I'd like a taste. The girl he wore that ring for had no idea what she was missing out on.

"Sir, are you mocking me or stalking me?" I asked as he straightened to his full height. Maybe I had a type ... he was tall like the pirate.

"My wife didn't stick around long enough to obtain an annulment, so I made a few calls and tracked her down."

I covered a giggle with the back of the hand holding his rose. "Aw, does that make you sad? Of course, if your heart belongs to another worth wearing a ring for, does that make me the other woman?"

"Aw, does that make you sad?" he mocked.

"Burn." I grinned, glad to be without a mask as well as to see his face.

"In truth, this dinner sounded fun and I'm dying to see who you have to kiss nearly more than who the murderer is." He shifted behind me to give others access to the photos at the table. "Reach for the photo at the back and hand it over, please?"

I swallowed and did as he said. I'd not felt such a rush since my pirate had grabbed my waist with my breakdown and sternly ordered me not to put my faith in boys but to choose a man.

This man took the photo and asked another woman to pass the magnifying glass beside her. Holding the photo up to the light, he turned away from the group and looked through the magnifying glass, then grunted and said, "Just as I suspected."

The group stopped looking at the other photos and salivated for a turn with the one he had.

He laid the evidence back on the table, discreetly reached for my hand and guided us from the horde. "I hope you don't mind if I ask you a few questions? Standard procedure. You understand."

Yeah, maybe the pirate had awakened dormant desires last year and now I was a hot mess for a real man over guys my age. The corners of my lips twitched, and I marveled at his diversion as no one paid us mind when they busied mass speculating.

"Go right ahead," I told him.

"The hair they found at the scene was long. You're the only one wearing a hat."

I nearly snorted again. My 'hat' was nothing more than a jewel-encrusted miniature bowler hat on an alligator clip. A sarcastic, yet charming nod to the days of yore. The rest of my hair was pinned into intricate braids with curls peeking out of the fray.

"If I killed her, are you going to tell?" I simpered, casting my eyes up to his casting suspicion on me.

"If you did, will you be so easy to catch as this?"

"Did she piss you off?" I asked him. "Make too many demands of a married man?" I quirked my eyebrows with mirthful danger, playing now as the wife in our pretend marriage. "You're the only one not taking notes. I figured the note found in her possession might match your penmanship."

"Impossible. How could I be the killer when I only showed up on a whim? I don't have to take notes. Photographic memory. I've already memorized you. You're her therapist. Tell me, my lover must have spoken of me for you to suspect she was making demands. What did she say?"

"Smooth." I snickered. "You know that's a breach of doctor-patient confidentiality. I cannot discuss it."

Another man approached. My stomach dipped. *Was this the man I'd have to kiss?* My companion shook hands with him, and I could tell he wondered the same.

"Interesting seeing the two of you in the same conversation...." The suspicious gent took in our proximity.

"Why's that?" my friend asked.

"The evidence clearly points to an affair between her lover and her therapist. Quite the tangled web of intrigue you all have going."

"Oh, but, sir, this man was having an affair with someone else. I was merely treating his wife for depression after her discovering his infidelity. Naturally, I wanted to see him in my office. Both of them, to try and mend their relationship. Sure, we had a few solo sessions. Only because I sensed he needed pointers pertaining to her."

"If you'll not disclose the truth because of doctor-patient confidentiality, I will," my friend said. "The truth is, I never had a lover. That woman was delusional, chasing me about the city, causing issues with my wife after coming onto me at every turn. How could I not look suspicious when she framed me to be? What my therapist isn't saying is that my wife and I were separating. I'm celibate."

I accidentally laughed, then cleared my throat, looking instead to the bubbles in his champagne flute rather than the man questioning us.

"Uh, huh ... I'm onto you both." Ah! A detective! "Mark my words, I'll bring you in before tonight's over. Both of you."

"The plot thickens," I murmured when he walked away with his eyes on us. "Two criminals in one murder mystery dinner? Is such a thing done?"

"He evidently thought so," my companion observed.

As the evening wore on, I worried that I'd missed my window.

"What if I've confused my partner in crime by chilling with you?" I peered up at the suave charmer who was now anything but a hot dork. Sure, I could've asked his name, but I didn't want to because I might fall into temptation from cravings the pirate had started inside me. "We shouldn't be here together," I added.

"How could I stay away? I was honest. I never touched her. I'm celibate."

"Including your wife?" I grinned.

"Why do you think she's so desperate? She doesn't do it for me. Even now she's watching you and wondering what it is about you that she cannot compare with. See?"

"Huh?" I looked around.

"Over my shoulder. I feel her eyes like a *knife.*" His eyes flared on the word like a cheesy clue. My smile erupted. I looked to the floor because there weren't any women behind him. "And ... if you don't tell ... I won't." A photograph with red strands of hair and evidence markers appeared in my eye-line.

"Holy crap. Does that mean *I'm* the killer?" I whispered. He tucked the photo away and his fingers brushed mine still clutching the rose.

"Coat closet, five minutes. If you don't show, I'll reveal you for the killer you are."

When he left, I tingled with wonder and bewilderment. He couldn't be my make-out partner. What should I do? Pretending with him was far too easy. The information for my character had said that my lover would be at table five sporting a red handkerchief. There were two men at table five wearing red pocket squares, a third donning a red ascot. If I'd told my new friend about that, would he have worn one just to screw with me? Seemed he was turning this whole mystery dinner into a thicker plot. Wherever Julie was, I'd bet she was panicking behind the scenes.

At the evidence table, my parents argued over one of the photos. I seized the moment to fade out of the ballroom and trot toward the coat room. How predictable and cliché.

A hand shot from somewhere at my side and yanked me before I reached the closet. Another hand came over my mouth to stifle my scream. "Shh. Shhhh. It's me. Who wants a corny tryst in a coat closet?"

I smiled against his hand as my eyes adjusted to the darkness in the *janitor*'s closet. My heart thundered in my ears. I should have smelled chemicals and cleaning products. I smelled him and reality blurred as he lowered his hand from my lips to my hip. "What about the actors? My rich make-out partner? Won't we throw off the plan?"

"Where's the fun in making everything so easy? Besides, without evidence, who says we had anything to do with it? Did you kill her?" he tested. His features were a shadow hovering so close I could touch his aura if I wanted. I wanted to very much.

"Did *you*?"

"If I were a killer, would it matter?" His mouth was closer than I expected as he dipped his head. I gasped, and he ran his nose against mine.

"No, it wouldn't," I breathed like a twisted confession.

More than my heart pounded as every area I denied came alive and gravitated until his arms wrapped my waist. The rose fell from my palm to the floor as his fingers traveled up to my exposed shoulder blades. My hands found his cheeks and navigated up to his hair as I let him seal the centimeters that separated us. Hot lips, no excess saliva, the stroke of his very perfect tongue coaxing mine into bad behavior ... I moaned. When he did, too, his mouth moved from my lips down my jaw like he'd been longing to do so all along. He nudged my chin with his nose, so I'd allow him access to my throat.

"Ohhh ...."

If this were scripted, would I feel less convicted for enjoying this so much?

"Pull harder," he urged as I dug my nails into his hair. I did as he said, but found I pushed his head so that his mouth kept traveling down to my collarbones. He kissed across them like he was pleased with their structure, and I felt drunk; heavy, rubbery, limp with longing to the point that he had to hold me tighter. "You're so beautiful, Kinsley."

"So are you. So much hotter than a dork."

"Do you know who I am?" he asked.

"Please, don't tell me! This can't happen again, and you have that ring on for her. I'm so bad for kissing you, but I can't help it."

"You're so good at it, I can't help indulging in being touched after waiting for so long for someone who doesn't want me."

"Oh, trust me, she'll want you," I managed through huffs between more kisses.

"I don't want them to find us." His confession enthralled me. I didn't want them to either, nor did I want to admit how I wanted so much more.

"You're a great actor," I mumbled just before his mouth sealed mine shut for another deep dive.

"Am I? Are you?" he breathed between pulls from my lips as we adjusted angle after sinful angle of enjoyment I hated myself for. I'd never felt like falling into bed with a total stranger in my life. I'd never kissed a stranger or hidden inside of a janitor's closet to do so. I wasn't a bad girl. I was nearly a virgin, and yet I felt like a full-grown woman in the arms of the man holding me the way the pirate had held me.

I knocked his glasses to the floor. The clip holding my curls fell, then the braids I'd wrapped around my crown dropped to my back as his hands unraveled this carefully crafted facade. "I have to know how long your hair is," he whispered.

"No!" I shoved him back. He gasped like I'd slapped him. "Is that what you're doing? Investigating me? How do I know you're not a cop just using me?"

His hand slapped over my swollen lips when we heard the clacking of heels in the corridor just outside our hiding place. The scripted actors headed for the coat closet. My tongue danced all over the palm silencing me to make him remove his fingers, but his other hand wrapped around my waist and yanked me against his firm torso. *Oh, my gosh, yes, I loved being grabbed! I was a twisted woman with no other explanation!*

"How do I know you're not seducing me to gain answers?" he asked. "You assume I want to see your hair for the case, but perhaps your mistake is thinking I don't have a real interest in you." His voice was a low decibel that reverberated to the core of my belly.

"You aren't allowed to be interested in me outside of this place. I love someone and so do you." I knew the pirate was who I wanted, and this man reminded me of why to the point of longing beyond lust. I missed that damn pirate like a sock losing a match. Nothing else fit or looked quite right. This man had that same something. That's all this was. Had to be!

"Is that why you kiss me like you shouldn't?" His lips grazed mine slow and disciplined, as if

I'd been the only one dizzy with desire moments ago.

"Is that why *you* kiss me like you really are a married man enjoying this for every second you can?" I growled and nipped one of his lips between my teeth hard enough to give pain without blood.

He cursed and returned the favor.

I gasped. "How dare you!"

"How dare *you!* I'm not allowed to be interested in anyone outside of this place, not because I'm married. Because I'm dangerous."

Dangerous? Was this part of his character or real?

Excitement mingled with trepidation in the pit of my stomach.

Too late I realized all my hair hung loose cascading down my back. His fingers teased the tendrils apart like he had any right to do so.

"What the hell?" I demanded loud enough that we'd be heard, then pushed at his chest. Rather than give the space I'd forced, he seized my mouth with his to silence me, and when his tongue met mine, I kissed him back knowing that this was how we *should* be caught: red-handed, heat-of-passion, anger, desire, *oh gosh he tasted good!* I held him tight for every dwindling second I'd never get back. Tonight was amazing and I'd never forget him!

Bottles crashed to the ground. His fingers dug into my hair with one greedy hand while the other molded to my back and kneaded my flesh like a sweet massage so contrary to his lips locked on mine like a lion pinning his prey to the death.

My nails dug into his scalp to punish him for his unacceptable behavior, for unleashing desires too soon, for belonging to someone else and making me miss the man I'd put in the past with my aching heart after we'd parted! Now, those emotions were back worse than before! His fault!

The door ripped open.

"You!" said the man with the red ascot. "I've searched everywhere and here I find you in the arms of another man!" *Well, hell. Was this dude waiting in the coat closet?* Insults spit from his mouth featuring yellowing teeth and a graying mustache while my killer kisser felt the floor for his glasses, then allowed me to huddle in his arms.

Had Julie lost her mind? This nasty guy looked my dad's age! His scorned anger didn't appear contrived. I couldn't help cuddling closer to the man protecting me when the detective at the socialite's side grabbed his arm to keep him in check. We shared eye-contact. On with the show!

Remembering my part and needing to redeem myself somehow, I shoved the man in my grip away and slapped him across the face as if I'd kissed him against my will; hard enough to leave a handprint and the sting in his memory.

His hand fired to his cheek, and he pretended for the crowd well enough, but his eyes gleamed like someone memorizing the details in my face while he relished the pain in his.

The ultimate triumph spread through his lips at ruining my disguise. He pointed at me and lifted my hair clip off the floor. "It was Miss Scarlett in the janitor's closet with a poisoned hair pin!"

"What?!" I gaped in shock I didn't feign.

The angry lover's lips dropped open, revealing a white, plaque-coated tongue I was *sooo* grateful I'd hadn't tangled with.

The detective shouted that my partner-in-crime prove his accusation. He seized me by my elbow— which I hate— as we followed my make-out man into the ballroom. He went to the table with the evidence and produced two photos, one being the shot he'd stolen. I smirked at his disheveled hair and tux, lips smeared and colored in my lipstick, glasses a mite crooked. The hot dork was back. The red rose boutonniere peeked from his breast pocket once more, a few petals askew. If that was how he looked, I was likely as hot a mess on the outside as he'd turned my insides!

"Long red hair." My kisser pointed. "And a single purple feather just like the ones beneath the jewels on her clip. Symptoms of poison in the victim. She's wearing the murder weapon in plain sight!"

"You framed her when you stole her!" ascot man accused. I cringed at the floor and side-eyed the hot guy. He didn't bat an eye, just stared confidently at the snubbed snob.

My father laughed and walked into the space between them, his cool gaze darting from Clark Kent to the socialite. "No one can steal what never belonged to you," he said cryptically. My body tensed at the private threat. Make-out man's eyes flared, a gorgeous smile splitting his suave indifference. The crowd made a collective 'oooh' at the blow dealt to an ego too huge to stay any longer. Ascot man stalked out of the ballroom. My father clapped slow and loud, grabbing the audience's attention once more like he held all the cards. He returned his attention to the disheveled devil. "Wearing the murder weapon, you say? Pray tell, where did Miss Scarlett *get* the purple clip she's wearing tonight?" Daddy produced a photo Julie had taken of us before showtime. Before Mom removed her clip and insisted I needed a little something in my hair. "Is it possible she was framed by none other than her older sister?"

Bum. Bum. Bum.

How had I missed this?

The crowd gasped and looked at my mother. I beamed when she released her long, curly red hair. She walked with the grace of a model to the middle of the silent crowd. Her unwavering attention settled on my accuser. Without turning, she reached over to twist a lock of my hair around her finger. I blushed, knowing, in addition to everyone else, my parents saw how hot the tryst with the wrong man had been.

"Sir, do you know the difference between her hair and mine?" Mom asked him, her glare inspecting him like he'd stolen her favorite jewelry.

He stood in wait, undaunted, obviously unashamed of stealing the show and mussing my appearance.

"The hair in the photo has natural spiral curl to it. Her hair is wavy because it was braided. Any woman knows a curl from a wave, so you've just played like a man in a woman's game."

Another collective 'oooh' sounded through the room.

"Framed by my own sister?" I cupped my swollen—*guilty*—lips, needing this to end.

At the detective's behest, fake police escorted my mother from the ballroom. My father collected the prize. In an alcove, Julie's hands flailed where she stood with a small group of other drama students questioning how they'd ruined the real murder plot they'd created. I heard her saying, "I told you that you'd make a mistake if you didn't outline everything and lay the right clues. Because of your inability to follow instructions, Kinsley kissed the wrong guy and the donor withdrew his donation! Thank goodness we had anonymous donation at the last minute or else we'd be a laughingstock!"

Hmm ... he'd owned up to being rich. Was this his way of saying my kiss was worth paying for?

Smiling to myself, I walked slowly down the hall, this time without a hand reaching out to yank me into a closet. I did, however, find the red rose boutonniere sitting just outside of the janitor's closet like a memento. I lifted the flower and headed for the outdoor balcony overlooking Tampa Bay.

Though I expected him to come from the shadows, I knew he wouldn't. The pirate, however, did filter through my mind with a renewed ache more acute than ever before. I hoped the hot dork would speak to the one he waited for and that she'd give him another chance to prove what an amazing person he really was. I also prayed my pirate would come back into my life when the time was right.

A longing sigh escaped my still-inflamed lips as I plucked the rose playing, *he loves me, he loves me not.* I tossed the petals into the ocean like a wishing well, the last petal landing on *he loves me.*

If only ....

WHEN LOVE IS A KILLER...

DON'T CLOSE
YOUR
EYES

Lynessa Layne

USA TODAY BESTSELLING AUTHOR

1 | ♂ - Don't Close Your Eyes

One Year Prior

MURDER WAS NEVER MY **intended occupation.**

Twenty-seven stories below, the Jose Gasparilla anchored in the center of the glittering water of Tampa Bay. Through a scope, I searched scores of smaller boats dotted around the majestic pirate ship until spotting the bright yellow cigarette boat dubbed *The Banana Hamick.*

I scribbled precise grid points onto a small notepad, shook my head.

This idiot can't spell *hammock*, yet stole two million worth in cocaine?

The take, disguised as cheesy gold coins, brimmed from an open treasure chest at his feet where he stood waving to the crowds gathered onshore.

I rolled my eyes and collapsed the scope.

Too easy. Where was the challenge, adrenaline, thrill of the hunt? Why hire me to kill this arrogant prat when a Dade City meth head would do the deed for a fraction of the price?

As I locked my office, a lone janitor paused his vacuuming.

"Wow!" he gushed. "Great costume, Mr. King. Enjoy wooing the wenches at Gasparilla. You'll have a hard time keeping them away."

"Thanks." I chuckled. "But I plan on enjoying the festival from the safety of a parade float." And sharp shooting from a crow's nest. I boarded the elevator. "There's a bucket of beads calling my name. Cheers, mate."

He waved as the doors closed. I leaned against the wall and fished a Bowie knife from my coat to check my eyeliner in the shine. Coal smudged beneath my finger when the elevator halted only five floors down.

"What the?" My words died as the doors divided on leather pants, round hips, corset, cleavage, slender throat, parted lips. The knife fell to my side while my mouth dried and fell open.

"Whoa!" She backed away. Beautiful green eyes, clouded with smeared mascara, widened. "I didn't expect anyone else." She shook her head, top hat firmly in place. "I'll catch the next one." "Nonsense, I don't mind sharing," I said, swallowed.

"That's okay," she said, "I'd rather be alone. Thank you."

The doors closed, but I shoved the blade between them, sliced them apart.

"Oh, no!" Her palm shot out while she stumbled back. "No! No, thank you! You go!"

"Wait. It's not what it looks like!"

"You leave, or I'll call the cops!"

"No, love, I didn't mean to use the bloody knife to open the lift! Gah! I mean elevator!" After living in the United Kingdom, certain words still slipped out.

High-heeled boots dashed behind the vacant reception desk. "I mean it!" she yelled. Fingers fumbled with the phone until the receiver clattered off the edge. "Oh, shit!" She sprinted down the hallway, tested office doors like a bimbo in a B-movie. The cell phone in her hand made little sense considering the phone she'd left dangling from the desk.

"Look, I'm leaving!" I pressed the elevator button for the next floor down. "You have nothing to fear!" I sheathed the knife. Pathetic girl. I ought to shake some sense into her! Show her how to escape a killer rather than cornering herself!

I shouldn't have gone after her. I didn't allow her to know I was, but no way I'd risk a police report bearing my description when I had a target to paint. The hell if I'd forego tonight's bounty when I relished ridding the world of that stupid criminal, retrieving the drugs and taking his boat as a bonus.

Exiting the elevator, I jogged back upstairs into the reception area. I padded across the lobby to re-cradle the screeching phone receiver. In the silence a woman's voice drifted as a distant echo. The lavatory!

Office doors were locked tight. Darkness showed beneath sets of closed vertical blinds subtly shifting with the blowing air conditioning.

Every whispered step closer to her amped up an adrenaline rush so exhilarating, I refused to heed the voice of reason shouting at me to flee as if I were prey.

My ear pressed to the door of the ladies' room. Overhead, a florescent light twitched. The buzz mixed with the young woman's voice leaching through the wood.

"Daddy, something—" She strangled a sob. "—awful happened at the festival!" Sob. "Nate, he, well … gosh … I have no idea where to begin or what to do!" Whiny, squeaky, hoarse cry. I jerked away from the wretched pitch before braving the door with my ear again. Throat clearing. Sniffling. Stronger tone. "Look, I'm okay. Emotional, but okay. My phone is dying. If you can't reach me, don't freak out. I might stop at a friend's place before I come home. Wanted you to know. Love yo u."

The beep of disconnection echoed off the tile walls. Unable to see her, I assumed the smack afterward was her phone against the granite countertop.

"Stupid, Kinsley! Stupid! Stupid! Stupid!" She shouted as if her voice might shatter the mirror. I cursed under my breath.

Silence. Sniffles. Lower tone.

Kinsley ....

I pressed harder to hear her, hoping she wouldn't scream again. She released a heavy exhale. "Okay, Kins. Quit being a coward. Call the cops. Let them deal with those creeps and the psycho with the knife, then go home. No one will know it was you. Totally anonymous." Shit. Cops?

Anger scorched my gut as I clutched the door handle. Was I the psycho with the knife? I hadn't done anything!

She blew her nose, sniffled again. I lost my give-a-damn and strode to the lift.

Let the foolish girl report a pirate in a building! The police had thousands to sort through tonight. She wasn't the daft fool, I was in thinking her fear mattered. Screw taking the stairs. I had nothing to hide!

I pounded the call button, pulled my pocket watch and cursed about how long the damn thing took to travel back upstairs. The halves of my watch snapped shut in my fist at the sound of her gasp.

"You said you were leaving," she said.

"And you said I was a psycho with a knife. Therefore, we are both liars." The lift arrived with a ping. I kept my back to her as I boarded, then turned with a scowl on my face to inspire something real for her to fear. "I came to check on you, however, I now find it best to leave you to your assumptions. Good evening." And good riddance.

Under my unconcealed disdain, her eyes dimmed with shame. They weren't a mess anymore, but her nose was pink. The color bled into her cheeks.

"You followed me?" Dumb question.

"Did you need to go downstairs then? Because I do." I stabbed the 'door close' button.

What the hell? I jerked when the girl rushed inside just before the doors sealed. She reached for the panel of numbers. Without thought, I threw my arm out to block her.

She yanked back. "What the hell?"

"Your makeup was a mess before I startled you."

"What?"

"Your eyes." I gestured with one hand, pocketed the other. "You fixed them, but your mascara was all over your face. Before I came along. Wasn't me you needed to call the cops about. What happened tonight?"

She stared, her only movement a swallow and an artery jumping at her throat. She'd stopped breathing. Several red splotches painted her chest and neck that had nothing to do with embarrassment.

"Please answer the question."

Her chest fell with a harsh exhale of all that trapped air. "No. It's none of your business. Why are you carrying a knife like that in a place like this?"

My head angled. Was that all she could think of? My knife?

"Perhaps this should be the business of the one carrying the knife. You see, love." My hand rested on my costume. "In case you couldn't tell, I'm also attending a festival and plan on protecting myself while I'm there."

"You use Mace to protect yourself at a festival, not a machete."

The space filled with my unexpected laughter. "Pepper spray? Is that what you used to fend off the bloke who left those fingerprints on your arm?"

She gasped and slapped her palm over the exact spot. A pink glow expanded up her temples.

My jaw clenched and lifted while I stood straight to look down on her.

"Who hurt you?"

Her gaze collected worry as she studied our confines with the dawning of a cornered creature cursing her stupidity.

"It's not like that," she argued.

"Then what is it like?" I all but growled. The thief in the Banana Hamick may not be tonight's only target.

"I don't want to talk about it. I don't even know you."

Determined, she reached around me for the button. Again, I prevented her by stepping between her and the column altogether.

"Ugh! Come on!" she pleaded.

"Hey. If someone did something, I'd rather take care of it than not. You're safe with me, but don't protect some asshole."

She narrowed her eyes with a mute implication that I was the asshole for the moment. A brave sign she was willing to test my word.

"Nothing happened. Not in the manner you're thinking."

"Right." I clenched my jaw as I held firm. "We're not moving until you elaborate."

She drilled a scowl through my skull like her problem was hers alone. I stalled, allowed silence to expand the interrogation. She caved in less than a minute. "Fine. My boyfriend stood me up. I put on this stupid outfit because he loves Gasparilla. We arranged to meet three hours ago. I waited for two-and-a-half past that and admitted defeat."

"How did you end up here?"

"Good grief," she spat. "You want my life story, too? My father works here. So, you see, I was running to Daddy because my boyfriend hurt my wittle feelings. Happy now? I guess I should apologize for wounding your precious pride."

On an aggravated whistle, I hammered the button for the car park, then balled my sweaty hands inside the deep pockets of my pirate coat. If she were going to a different floor, she could press her own button for grating against mine.

"I'm sorry." She deflated.

"So, pout about it."

"Hey, you asked! I told you I didn't want to talk about it." She peeked at the red indicator, then pressed the next floor. "I don't need your trash." Seconds later, she jumped off like I was diseased. The doors closed, and I let them. I didn't need her garbage either. What did that little wench even matter? Leave her be! But I couldn't. Nor could I define why I shattered the silence on a slew of curses and stabbed a button three floors further down.

The moment the doors cracked, I darted into the stairwell. Racing heels clacked down the stairs. The concrete echoed with her hoarse sobs. I let the heavy metal door slam. She cursed as I heard her turn to jog the other way.

"Come on! It's only me!" I shouted up through the space where the railing wound around each level. The clattering paused. She leaned over from two floors above.

"Oh, and that's supposed to make me feel better?" she shouted. "Leave me alone."

"Yeah? And leave you at the mercy of a pervert lurking in dark places like these?" I snapped back.

"You mean like you?" she asked.

"I mean like the wanker you're covering for! Blast!" I leapt out of the way as she spit. Her saliva missed me and continued down the fifteen remaining flights. A moment later, a steel door slammed. No more footsteps. Hell no! Now it was personal.

I ripped the exit open and stormed to the elevator, mashed the button. The floor indicator ticked down. Once the doors split, I half-expected her not to be inside, but there she stood, hands curled around the bar against the back wall. Her glare blazed with anger, but there flashed something challenging. Mine mirrored the sentiment.

"I didn't deserve that." I gave her my back while I pressed for the garage once more. "Any of it."

"The hell you didn't," she stammered. "You shouldn't have left the elevator, I told you to leave me alone, and I'm not covering for anyone. You were chasing me for goodness sakes!"

My eyes flared, and I turned with incredulous disbelief at her foolish bravery. "Chasing you? Shame on me for trying to be chivalrous."

"Chivalrous?" She scoffed. "You call that chivalry when you practically wore the inconvenience of all this upstairs? I wasn't planning on you interrupting me either, bud."

I shook my head, unable to help my disgust. "No wonder your bloke stood you up."

She flinched like I'd slapped her. The heaving in her chest returned. Lunging forward, she halted our progress just to grate on my nerves, then twisted to face me, bucking-up. Her bravado soon wavered under my silent scrutiny.

"Young lady, I haven't time to play these childish games." I reached toward the panel. She jolted back against the column of buttons before melting down on the marble beneath our feet. Multiple floors lit, but that didn't strike me as much as her presumption that I'd strike her. Was I that scary?

"You're right." Her voice cracked as her face fell into her hands. "I deserved it. I'm a terrible girlfriend."

I hadn't an umbrella adequate for this absurd rain of emotion. With a sigh, I knelt and cupped my hands beneath her arms to lift her to her feet, bracing for the spit likely to splat in my eye.

"Forgive me if I scared you again, love, but why not spit in his face instead of mine?"

"Why would you assume I won't?" she asked in bitterness.

We stopped on the first of twelve additional levels. She stared at me, I stared at her until the doors closed once more. Interesting. She'd just conceded a perfect moment to escape. With eleven bloody floors to go, I prodded her places of pain.

"Let's pretend I believe you. Why meltdown over this bloke? Were you together long?"

"Long enough, or so I'd thought. I guess in light of tonight, we were together too long." She looked everywhere but at me. "I wasted so much time on him." Her eyes ran out of space and traveled up to mine, big, beseeching, apologetic. "I'm sorry I've wasted yours."

That look loaded the bullet in a mental game of Russian roulette.

Drop this pistol and leave the risk!

Fresh tears added to her a different vulnerability that unsettled my normal control. Even if I knew she was lying, I'd been an insensitive asshole. Fix it. But how?

The doors opened again. No way was I was doing this ten more times. I herded her from our cell to press the button for the other one. She argued the whole way out, bargaining for using the extra floors for contemplation.

"You mean for wallowing? There's nothing to contemplate. If something is finished, let it be, and move on," I commanded. The indicator counted from the parking level. The bell chimed, the doors split open, but she didn't budge.

"I'll wait for the next one," she said. "Thanks."

Pft! No way in hell I'd concede with the visual and emotional target she'd painted on herself. Add the foolish fight-or-flight responses, she was prime for the wrong prick. Not on my watch.

"Nonsense. Come now." Plying her was like taking a stubborn jackass for a walk. After another verbal battle with her attitude, the bloody doors that kept trying to pinch us, my patience snapped. I spun her and cinched her waist in my grip.

"Oh!" She gasped while she grabbed my shoulders. I somewhat lost my head as the ribbons crisscrossing the length of her spine danced like feathers in a bow over my fingertips. Her body shifted closer, whether I'd tugged her, or she'd leaned in, I couldn't say. I only knew I wasn't getting enough oxygen as her chest brushed mine. Her fingers laced together at the nape of my neck. My lips parted to release a long steady breath. Her eyelids fell a fraction as she watched. When I stroked my thumbs against her waist, she bit her lower lip as I felt a tremor travel through her having nothing to do with fear. Tension compounded as the doors sealed us inside the private cocoon. My tone firm yet gentle, I powered through.

"Look at me, love." Look at me, she did. Up close, her irises heated like the blood pounding my veins. My gaze strayed to her gnawed lip for relief.

I hardened my expression and resolve while I warred with pressing her against the wall to taste the cinnamon of her breath.

"Enough of this," I said almost to myself. "Don't waste your time drafting excuses for someone else's misbehavior. Quit looking for your father to coddle you. For the sake of your self-esteem, stop dating little boys. They've no fortitude." My mind clouded with dangerous inspiration while she searched my face. Angry tears glazed her eyes like puddles of gasoline while my desire sparked like a pyromaniac holding a Zippo lighter. One strike may cause a beautiful explosion.

No woman had ever looked at me like I had the power to put away her pain even though I'd had a hand in causing hers. Why did she?

"I swear," I whispered aloud what ought to remain in my mind, "you would be so strong with a real man." With me, I finished with my eyes.

She gasped, conflicted and offended. Her brows dipped while she read my eyes like she understood the words written in my mind. I sensed the same about reading hers. This young woman didn't need a kid causing drama. She needed the adrenaline rush of being shoved to the precipice of a cliff, then yanked back to safety by someone who couldn't resist her before he brought her to combustion.

"Come to Gasparilla with me," I blurted, mutinous against my priorities, my bad side, those who controlled me.

"No." She released a shaky breath.

Curse that damn word again!

She broke my grasp to push the garage button I'd neglected.

"I don't date strangers," she said like she'd hardened her own resolve.

"Perhaps you should."

She arched her eyebrow. "Nope."

"Coffee then?" I asked. "To get to know one another?" The floors ticked down like a time bomb closer to detonating and obliterating every conflicted second with her!

"The coffee shop is closed on Saturdays."

"I know. We don't have to go to this shop or the festival. We can go anywhere you want." I shifted to close the small distance between us, desperate to be near her once more, but she shook her head.

"I think you've gotten the wrong impression of me."

"Ditto."

She scrunched her nose. "No, I mean this." She added space between us and gestured to her attire. "This isn't me. For starters, I don't dress like a 'ho', I'm not easy and dating isn't that simple. I don't need a consolation prize. I need to get away from you."

Ouch! How could she say that when she'd been wanton in my grasp moments ago?

The lift opened on the parking garage. Humidity glued to our skin as thick and uncomfortable as the chemistry between us. We surveyed the dimly lit expanse. Few cars remained. She was lucky I was here, though my pride ached to hell.

"Great," I said. "I'm too complicated to give you consolation, nor do I date. I was merely softening the bruise to your ego." I propped one hand against the door. My other gestured she exit first. Under normal circumstances, I'd have relished wounding someone who'd wounded me, but I loathed the flush of pain in her expression. No different from what she'd done to me, but this stung.

"Anyone ever tell you what an asshole you are?" High heels hammered the concrete as she left.

I swallowed. "All the time, love."

"I hate this. I'm done with men and their drama. It's all the same. And you're ...." She trailed off in search of a word that might match how low I measured, inspecting me for flaws. Rosy blossoms on the apples of her cheeks betrayed her. That's right, love, I'm not alone in this inexplicable attraction and misery.

"I'm what?" I taunted. "Grown up? Mature? Too big a prick?" Better if she hated me to escape my attention. Safer for both of us.

"Too old?" The corners of her lips lifted like that mental Russian roulette revolver. Her expressive eyes spun the cylinder as I stared like a victim realizing too late his own number was up. Victorious knowing fired from her irises, nailing my contempt, bleeding my strength. She turned and stalked away, determined to hold the power over me tight in her little fist. Not so fast.

"You're not done. If you'd had a man instead of a boy, you'd be done with drama, because real men don't have time for theatrics. Nor do real men hurt women. You're finished with temperamental kids. Maybe ring me when you're not one anymore." I strolled behind her enjoying the line of her legs in Puss-in-Boots stilettos.

"What are you doing?" She spun so fast I stumbled into her. Her squeal echoed off the concrete pillars while I grabbed her to keep us both from falling. Warm hands wrapped around my neck. Fiery eyes blazed mine with accusation. Uh, huh. Two can play this game.

"Did you do that on purpose?" I grinned.

"Ha! You wish." She stabilized and threw a finger in my face. The weak girl vaporized to re-materialize into a dominating woman. Pure beauty. This young lady, Kinsley, was the Anne Bonny to my Calico Jack ... Kinsley King has quite the ring ....

"I asked you a question." She interrupted my reverie. "What are you doing?"

I blinked hard. What was I doing? Hell, what was I thinking?

"Dangerous to be alone in a parking garage at night dressed so sexy." I nodded toward her costume. "Here. Take this." I shrugged out of my pirate coat.

"Oh, the chivalry angle again?" She stared at my offering with a stubborn lift of her chin. When I raised my eyebrows, she grimaced and yanked the heavy crushed velvet from my hand. She shrugged into the sleeves much longer than her arms. Anne Bonny looked mighty adorable in my coat. Too adorable to sport such a venomous attitude.

"Lead the way," I told her.

She snorted. "I don't think so."

My finger rose this time. "I'm walking you to your car."

"Why? To put me in my car seat and buckle my belt?"

"If you need it, sure, but I figured you'd at least graduated to a booster seat." She was so frustrated I barely contained a grin. "In those heels, I bet you can even reach the pedals."

"Insults coming from Peter Pan in a Captain Hook costume? That's cute."

I winced like she'd burned me before my wicked smile spread. "Oh, come now, love. At least grant me a solid Captain Morgan."

"Yeah, I could use a few shots of rum after being around you."

I chuckled. She turned to keep walking. Her pace quickened. I kept up, and she grumbled as we narrowed in on a shiny green Civic. The unmistakable feeling of watching eyes skittered over my back, raising goosebumps on my neck. Glancing around like she sensed danger, too, she pulled the coat closed. Her eyes held mine for a ghost of a second. We were being observed. She rushed to her car with new urgency while I scanned for threats.

She had my knife. I'd rather not pull my pistol unless I had to. Improvisations formulated as she unlocked her car, the lights flashing once. I reached for her door, but she spun with a scolding index pointing at my face again. A great effort with the sleeve.

"No," she said. "You don't get to open my door. Funny how you don't have time for childish games, yet you're the one playing them."

"Am not—"

"Are, too. Know what I'm done with? Fear. Everyone knows boys have a fear of commitment. I shouldn't be heartbroken about being stood up. It's always coming as long as they're not allowed to. And here I have a man—" She poked my chest. "—arguing like a child while lecturing me like I'm the weak one, when he'd likely walk away for the same reasons? It takes real strength to hold out for what you want, so admit it. Which of us is weakest? Who's the kid? Be honest." "Whoa!" I stammered, amusement confiscated. Hers was, too.

What had this bloke done to her? Dumped her over sex? Forced her without permission after she'd changed her mind?

LYDIESSA LAYNE

Her finger stayed in place. I wrapped my hand around her fist and leaned in to convey the severity in my gaze. "You're wrong."

She snorted and speared my eyes with a dare to prove otherwise. "You're weak. You're afraid. You're all the same." Anne Bonny shoved me aside to open the car door by herself and plunked into the driver's seat. I grabbed the door before she closed me out. My bravado challenged, she was testing me, but I was too angry at my imagination and her comparing me to that boy.

"No," I measured, "I'm not. It's complicated. I'm complicated. I will say no more on the matter." But I wanted to!

"Ha! Well, that makes two of us. Walk the plank or call me when you've grown up." She tossed her hat at my feet before yanking the door from my grasp.

"I need a number for that!" I shouted as she drove away. The peal of tires cut off my retort.

No more banter. No more ball-busting bitchiness or vulnerable softness, sweet perfume, coconut-scented lotion. No more cinnamon on her breath near my lips. No more Anne Bonny and Calico Jack!

I cursed the empty silence while my eyes drifted to the ground. How to proceed? She wanted proof, action over words. Impossible for too many reasons, but if I failed to act, someone else would, or worse, she'd ignore my wisdom and run back into the arms of someone who may have attacked her in his need to have what she'd refused. Did he stand her up before or after? Or had someone else attacked her after she'd been stood up? Why would she protect them?

Who the hell cares because she's gone!

Gone!

Why did she matter?

Was I a bloody masochist because she made my palms sweat?

After long years on the job, nothing rattled my cage. She not only pried at the bars of my prison but sent an earthquake through the very foundations setting free the possibilities of life. I was so damn screwed.

I grabbed the hat and dusted off the brown felt. A burst of bay breeze carried her scent from the accessory. Instead of emasculating myself and lifting the perfume to my nose, I trudged to the Range Rover to drive away from here and this experience. I opened the door as a shield, yanked the gun from the holster at my back, pulled back the hammer, and spun to take aim on another pirate.

"Freeze!"

"Shit! Easy, King!" Joey cried. My personal protective detail's hands flew up beside his temples. The feather on his cavalier hat waved in the wind. My barrel poised to fire two inches from his face, but he whistled with the wry grin of a card sharp holding a royal flush. He may as well have been. He had enough to run to my superiors and out my interlude with the girl.

"You're mighty brave, mate." I lowered the gun and thumbed the safety in place. "Lucky you didn't come any closer."

Joey dabbed sweat from his brow. "I'd say you're the brave one. She's mean. Aren't you lucky I caught these in case you needed a witness?" He held his phone up as I holstered the Sig. His display lit with several images of Bitchy Bonny flaying my heart. I masked my excitement. "She looks cute and harmless," he said, "but for a second, I thought I'd need to step in and defend you. Especially when you armed her. She has the coat. The coat has the knife."

"Maybe I prefer a fair fight," I joked. In truth, I was glad she kept the weapon in case she needed to castrate whoever left the prints on her arm.

Joey chuckled as he emailed the photos to my inbox, then deleted them until arriving on the final picture.

"The good news is … drum roll please …." His thumb scrolled. Kinsley's license plate centered on the screen. "Guess you got that number after all."

Regret replaced with promising reprisal as he sent the photo then hit delete.

"Ready to go hunting?" he asked.

My lips spread into a villainous smile. "Damn right."

About Lynessa Layne

Lynessa Layne is a native Texan from the small town of Plantersville. She's a fan of exploration, history, the beach (though she's photosensitive), Jesus, and America too (RIP Tom). Besides being an avid reader, she's obsessed with music of all types (hence her reference to Tom Petty). As a child, she created music videos in her mind and played Barbies perhaps a little longer than most with her little sister, not yet realizing she was writing and enacting stories all along.

Though she's put away the dolls, she now uses her novels as an updated, grown-up version of the same play.

Lynessa is also a certified copy editor and a member of Mystery Writers of America, with work featured by Writer's Digest and Mystery and Suspense Magazine. She has also graced the cover of GEMS (Godly Entrepreneurs & Marketers) Magazine and was a finalist for Killer Nashville's 2022 Silver Falchion Awards for Best Suspense and Reader's Choice.

For more visit lynessalayne.com and sign up for her newsletter, Lit with Lynnie and follow on social media:

https://www.facebook.com/authorlynessalayne

https://www.instagram.com/lynessalayne/

https://twitter.com/LynessaLayne

Writers like me depend on readers like you.
Please leave a positive review.
Thanks
♡ - *Lynessa*

Made in the USA
Middletown, DE
27 July 2024

57908658R00057